D0899977

Port Jefferson Free Library
100 Thompson Street
Port Jefferson, NY 11777

STAR WARS
FORCES OF DESTINY™
LEIA

Writers
Elsa Charretier & Pierrick Colinet

Artist
Elsa Charretier

Colorist
Sarah Stern

Letterer
Tom B. Long

Assistant Editor
Peter Adrian Behravesh

Editors
Bobby Curnow & Denton J. Tipton

ABDO Spotlight IDW Disney · LUCASFILM

ABDOBOOKS.COM

Reinforced library bound edition published in 2019 by Spotlight, a division of ABDO, PO Box 398166, Minneapolis, Minnesota 55439. Spotlight produces high-quality reinforced library bound editions for schools and libraries.
Published by agreement with IDW.

Printed in the United States of America, North Mankato, Minnesota.
092018
012019

THIS BOOK CONTAINS
RECYCLED MATERIALS

STAR WARS FORCES OF DESTINY—LEIA. JANUARY 2018. FIRST PRINTING.
© 2018 Lucasfilm Ltd. & ® or ™ where indicated. All Rights Reserved. © 2018 Idea and Design Works, LLC. All Rights Reserved. IDW Publishing, a division of Idea and Design Works, LLC. Editorial offices: 2765 Truxtun Road, San Diego, CA 92106. The IDW logo is registered in the U.S. Patent and Trademark Office. Any similarities to persons living or dead are purely coincidental. With the exception of artwork used for review purposes, none of the contents of this publication may be reprinted without the permission of Idea and Design Works, LLC.

Library of Congress Control Number: 2018945160

Publisher's Cataloging-in-Publication Data

Names: Charretier, Elsa; Colinet, Pierrick, authors. | Charretier, Elsa; Stern, Sarah, illustrators.
Title: Leia / by Elsa Charretier and Pierrick Colinet; illustrated by Elsa Charretier and Sarah Stern.
Description: Minneapolis, MN : Spotlight, 2019 | Series: Star wars: Forces of destiny
Summary: Leia wishes she could get her tauntaun to behave, but the stubborn creature is the least of her worries when they are separated from Han and Hera during a mission and come face-to-face with a wampa.
Identifiers: ISBN 9781532142949 (lib. bdg.)
Subjects: LCSH: Star Wars fiction--Juvenile fiction. | Space warfare--Juvenile fiction. | Women heroes--Juvenile fiction. | Extraterrestrial beings--Juvenile fiction. | Good and evil--Juvenile fiction.
Classification: DDC 741.5--dc23

Spotlight

A Division of ABDO
abdobooks.com

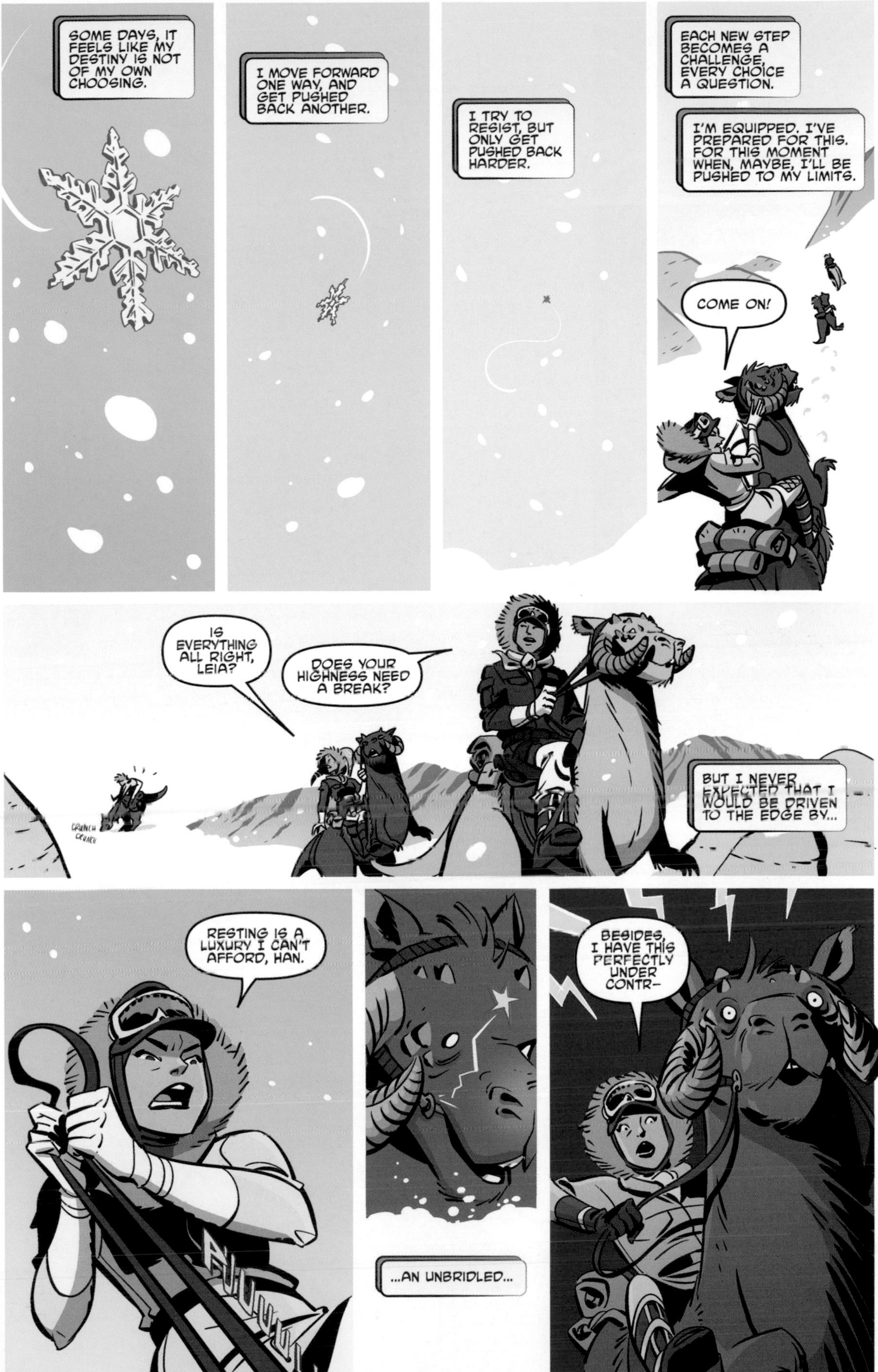

SOME DAYS, IT FEELS LIKE MY DESTINY IS NOT OF MY OWN CHOOSING.
I MOVE FORWARD ONE WAY, AND GET PUSHED BACK ANOTHER.
I TRY TO RESIST, BUT ONLY GET PUSHED HARDER BACK HARDER.
EACH NEW STEP BECOMES A CHALLENGE, EVERY CHOICE A QUESTION.
I'M EQUIPPED. I'VE PREPARED FOR THIS. FOR THIS MOMENT WHEN, MAYBE, I'LL BE PUSHED TO MY LIMITS.
COME ON!
IS EVERYTHING ALL RIGHT, LEIA?
DOES YOUR HIGHNESS NEED A BREAK?
CRUNCH CRUNCH
BUT I NEVER EXPECTED THAT I WOULD BE DRIVEN TO THE EDGE BY...
RESTING IS A LUXURY I CAN'T AFFORD, HAN.
PULLLL
...AN UNBRIDLED...
BESIDES, I HAVE THIS PERFECTLY UNDER CONTR–

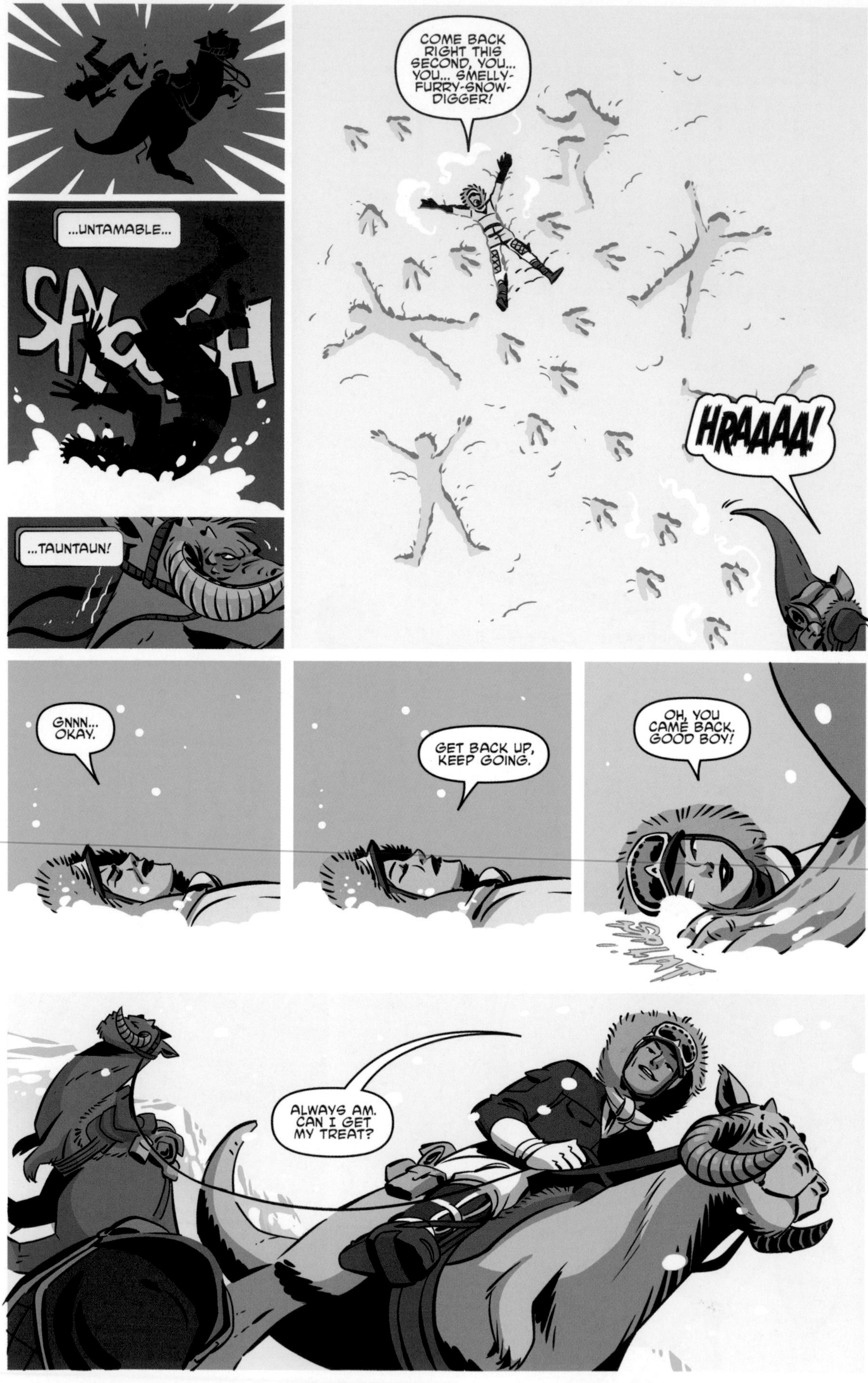
...UNTAMABLE...
SPLOOSH
...TAUNTAUN!
COME BACK RIGHT THIS SECOND, YOU... YOU... SMELLY-FURRY-SNOW-DIGGER!
HRAAAA!
GNNN... OKAY.
GET BACK UP, KEEP GOING.
OH, YOU CAME BACK. GOOD BOY!
ALWAYS AM. CAN I GET MY TREAT?

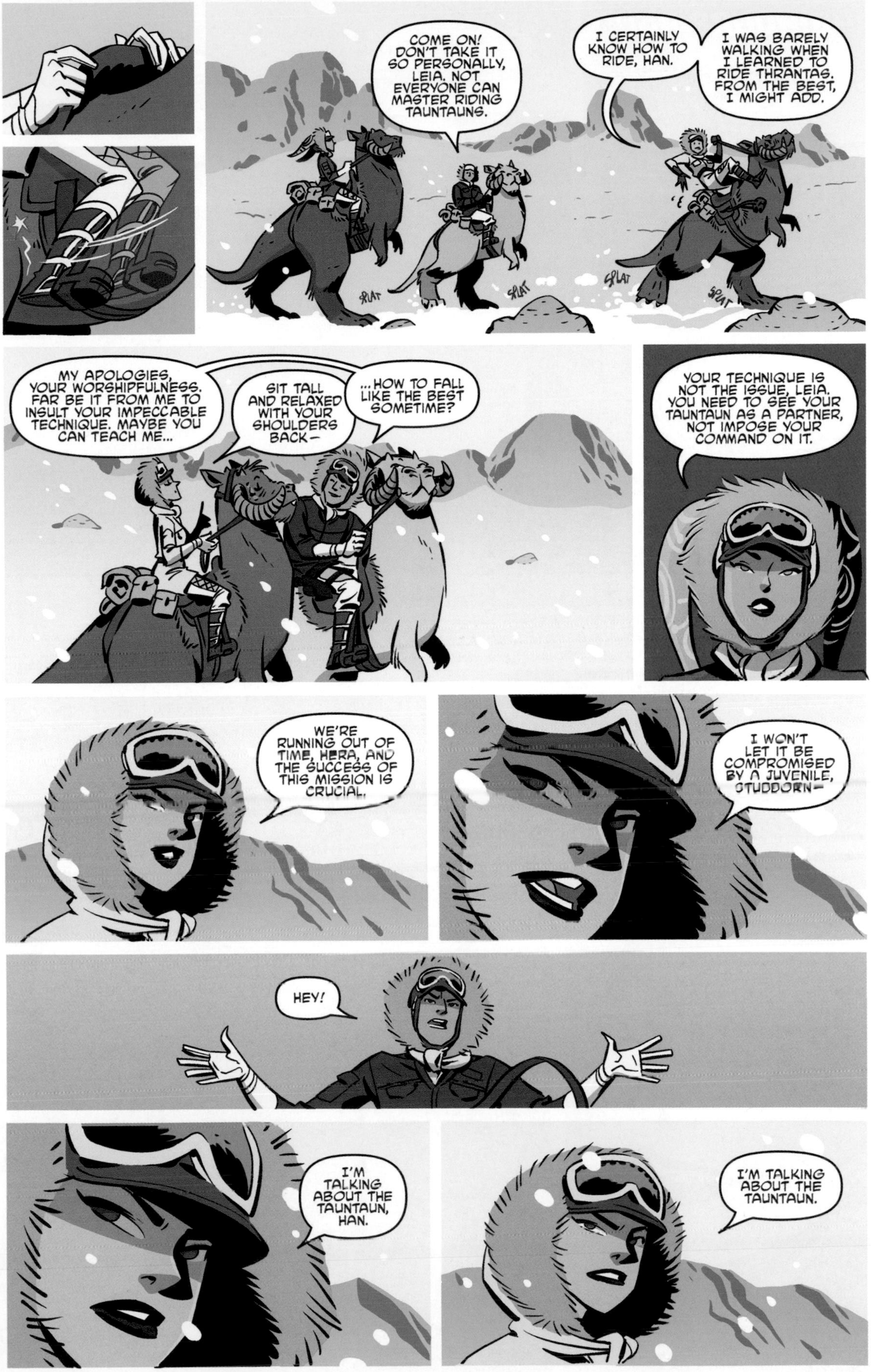
COME ON! DON'T TAKE IT SO PERSONALLY, LEIA. NOT EVERYONE CAN MASTER RIDING TAUNTAUNS.
I CERTAINLY KNOW HOW TO RIDE, HAN.
I WAS BARELY WALKING WHEN I LEARNED TO RIDE THRANTAS. FROM THE BEST, I MIGHT ADD.
SPLAT
SPLAT
SPLAT
SPLAT
MY APOLOGIES, YOUR WORSHIPFULNESS. FAR BE IT FROM ME TO INSULT YOUR IMPECCABLE TECHNIQUE. MAYBE YOU CAN TEACH ME...
SIT TALL AND RELAXED WITH YOUR SHOULDERS BACK—
...HOW TO FALL LIKE THE BEST SOMETIME?
YOUR TECHNIQUE IS NOT THE ISSUE, LEIA. YOU NEED TO SEE YOUR TAUNTAUN AS A PARTNER, NOT IMPOSE YOUR COMMAND ON IT.
WE'RE RUNNING OUT OF TIME, HERA, AND THE SUCCESS OF THIS MISSION IS CRUCIAL.
I WON'T LET IT BE COMPROMISED BY A JUVENILE, STUBBORN—
HEY!
I'M TALKING ABOUT THE TAUNTAUN, HAN.
I'M TALKING ABOUT THE TAUNTAUN.

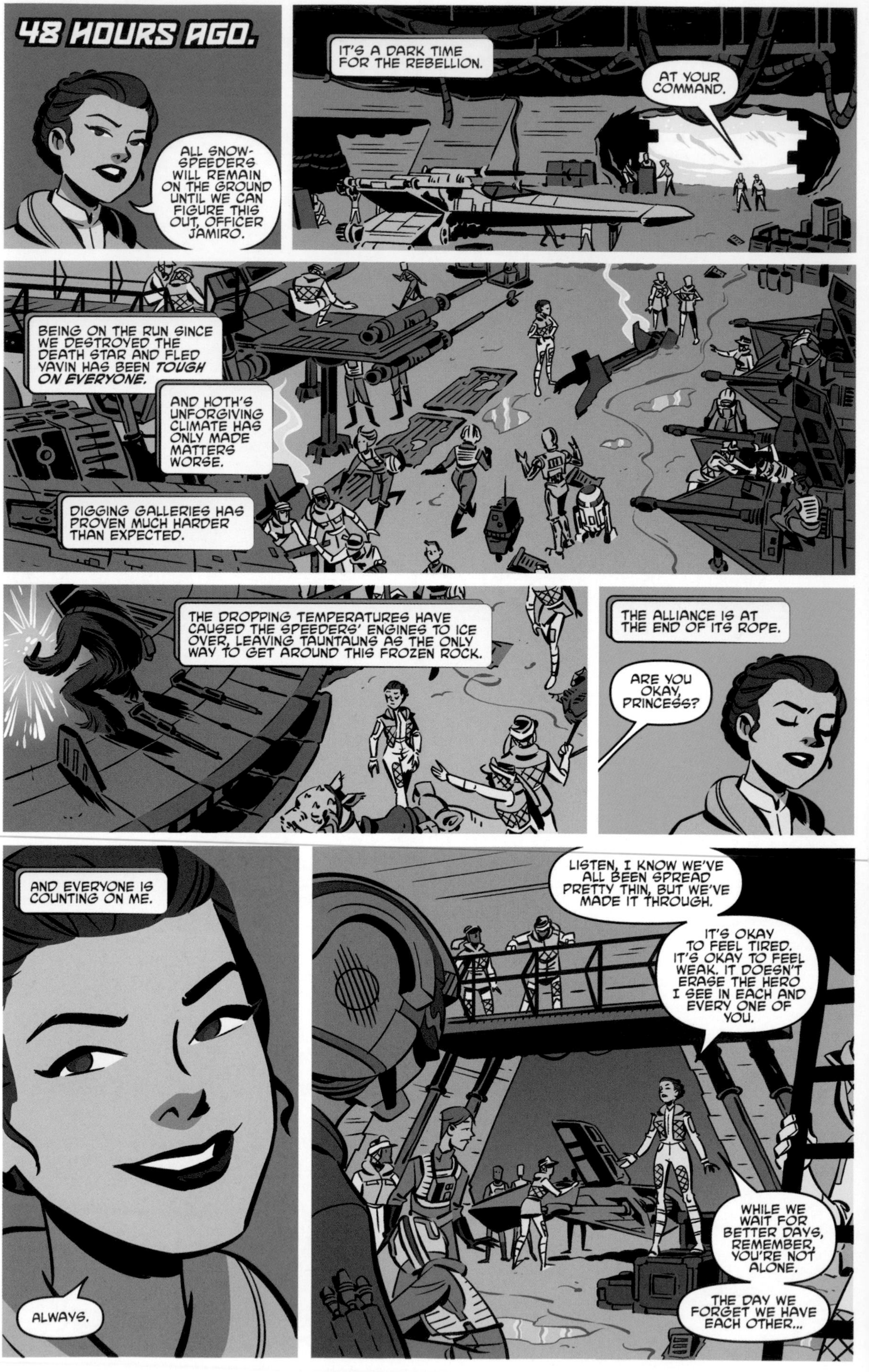
48 HOURS AGO.
ALL SNOW-SPEEDERS WILL REMAIN ON THE GROUND UNTIL WE CAN FIGURE THIS OUT, OFFICER JAMIRO.
IT'S A DARK TIME FOR THE REBELLION.
AT YOUR COMMAND.
BEING ON THE RUN SINCE WE DESTROYED THE DEATH STAR AND FLED YAVIN HAS BEEN *TOUGH ON EVERYONE.*
AND HOTH'S UNFORGIVING CLIMATE HAS ONLY MADE MATTERS WORSE.
DIGGING GALLERIES HAS PROVEN MUCH HARDER THAN EXPECTED.
THE DROPPING TEMPERATURES HAVE CAUSED THE SPEEDERS' ENGINES TO ICE OVER, LEAVING TAUNTAUNS AS THE ONLY WAY TO GET AROUND THIS FROZEN ROCK.
THE ALLIANCE IS AT THE END OF ITS ROPE.
ARE YOU OKAY, PRINCESS?
AND EVERYONE IS COUNTING ON ME.
ALWAYS.
LISTEN, I KNOW WE'VE ALL BEEN SPREAD PRETTY THIN, BUT WE'VE MADE IT THROUGH.
IT'S OKAY TO FEEL TIRED. IT'S OKAY TO FEEL WEAK. IT DOESN'T ERASE THE HERO I SEE IN EACH AND EVERY ONE OF YOU.
WHILE WE WAIT FOR BETTER DAYS, REMEMBER, YOU'RE NOT ALONE.
THE DAY WE FORGET WE HAVE EACH OTHER...

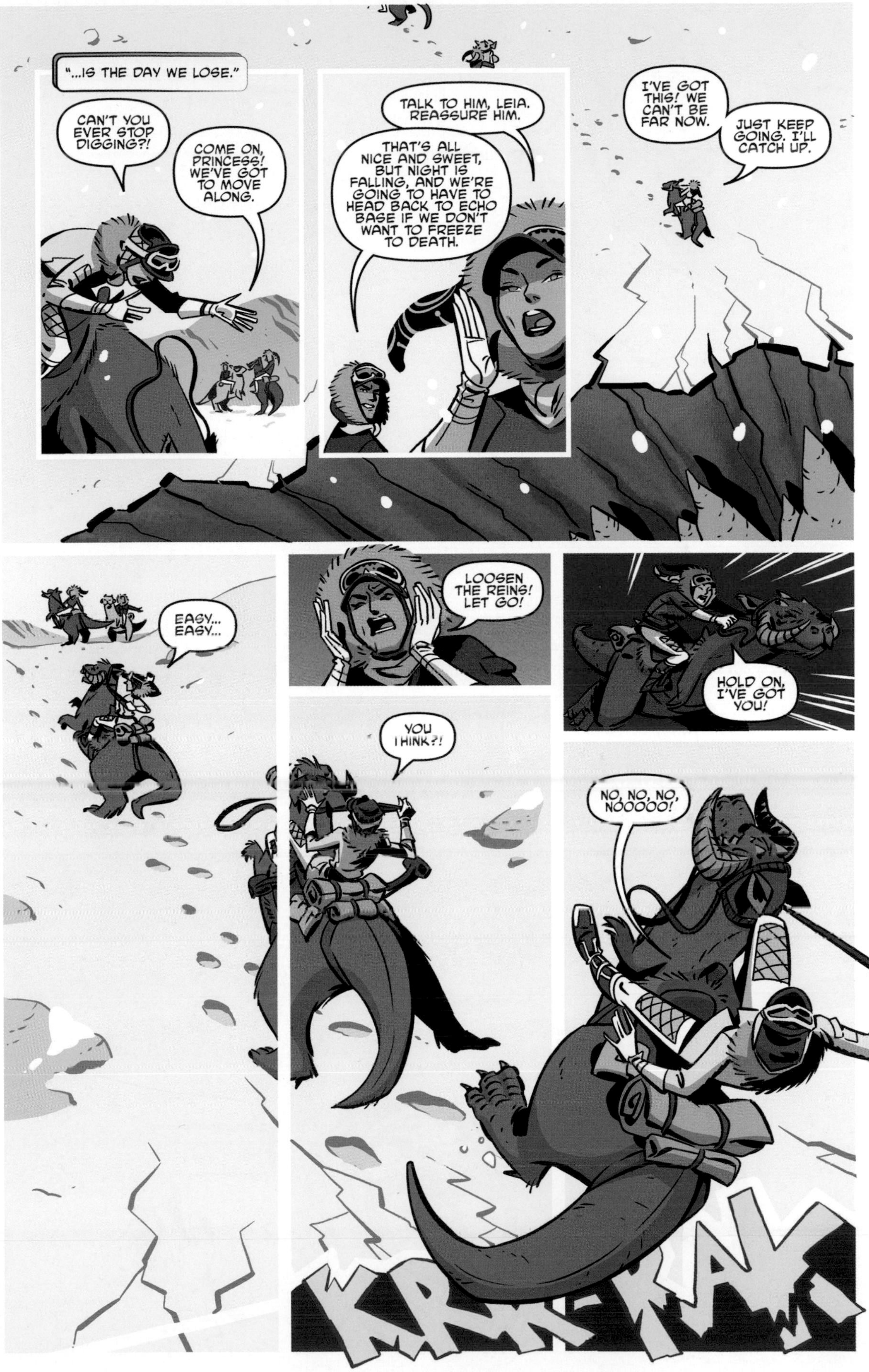
"...IS THE DAY WE LOSE."
CAN'T YOU EVER STOP DIGGING?!
COME ON, PRINCESS! WE'VE GOT TO MOVE ALONG.
TALK TO HIM, LEIA. REASSURE HIM.
THAT'S ALL NICE AND SWEET, BUT NIGHT IS FALLING, AND WE'RE GOING TO HAVE TO HEAD BACK TO ECHO BASE IF WE DON'T WANT TO FREEZE TO DEATH.
I'VE GOT THIS! WE CAN'T BE FAR NOW.
JUST KEEP GOING. I'LL CATCH UP.
EASY... EASY...
LOOSEN THE REINS! LET GO!
HOLD ON, I'VE GOT YOU!
YOU THINK?!
NO, NO, NO, NOOOOO!
KRRK-RAK!

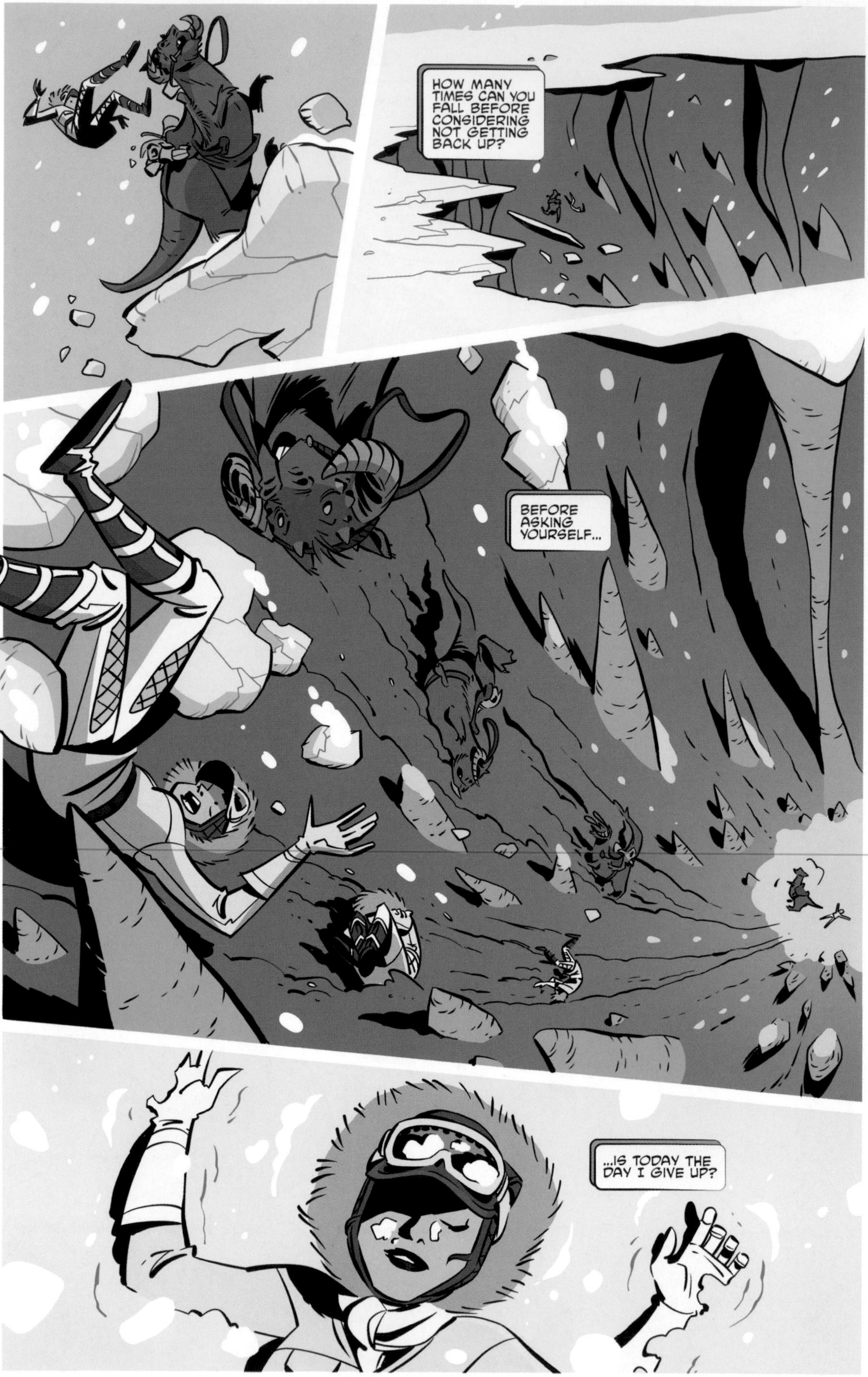
HOW MANY TIMES CAN YOU FALL BEFORE CONSIDERING NOT GETTING BACK UP?
BEFORE ASKING YOURSELF...
...IS TODAY THE DAY I GIVE UP?

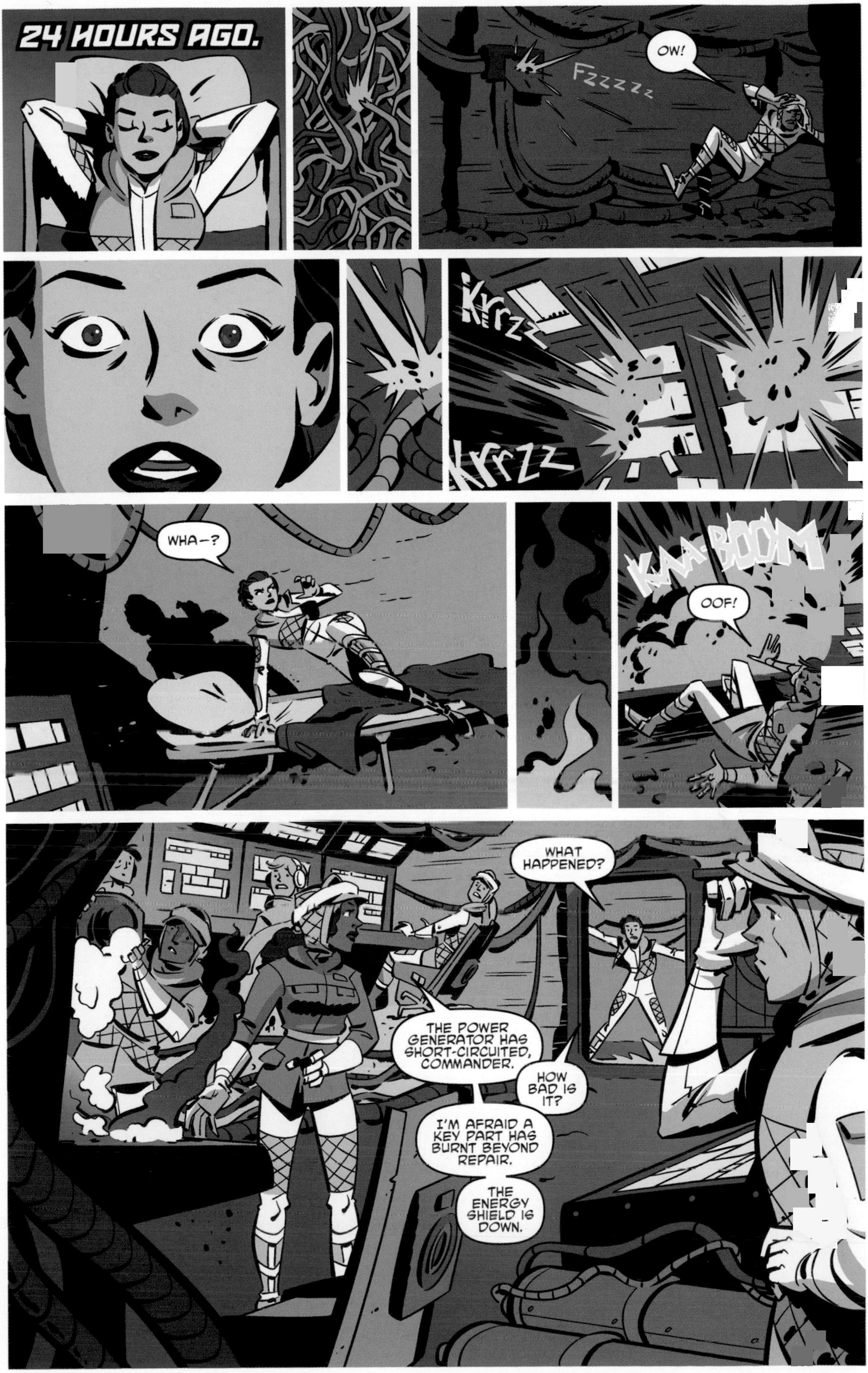
24 HOURS AGO.
OW!
Fzzzzz
Krrzz
Krrzz
WHA--?
KAA-BOOM
OOF!
WHAT HAPPENED?
THE POWER GENERATOR HAS SHORT-CIRCUITED, COMMANDER.
HOW BAD IS IT?
I'M AFRAID A KEY PART HAS BURNT BEYOND REPAIR.
THE ENERGY SHIELD IS DOWN.

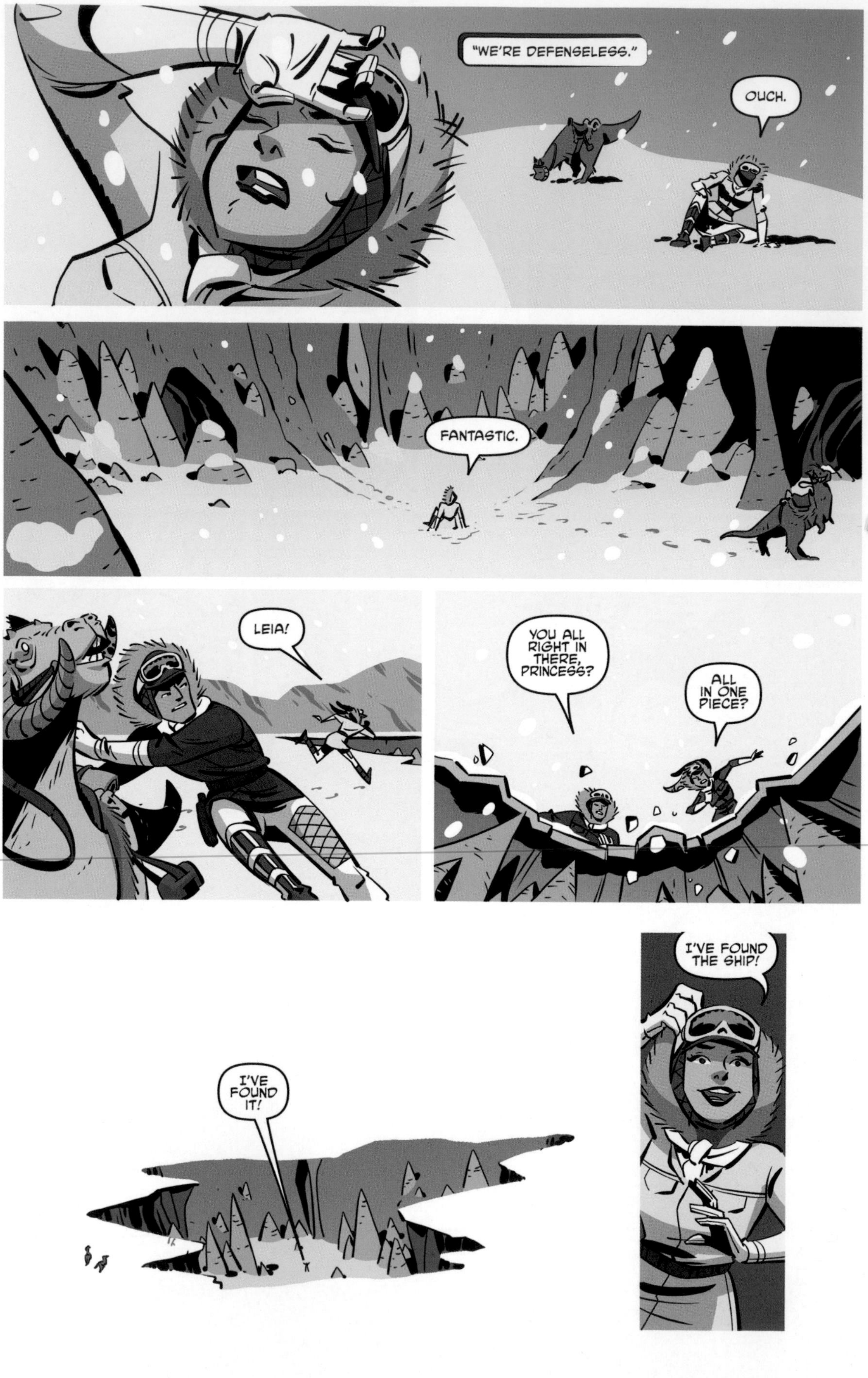
"WE'RE DEFENSELESS."
OUCH.
FANTASTIC.
LEIA!
YOU ALL RIGHT IN THERE, PRINCESS?
ALL IN ONE PIECE?
I'VE FOUND IT!
I'VE FOUND THE SHIP!

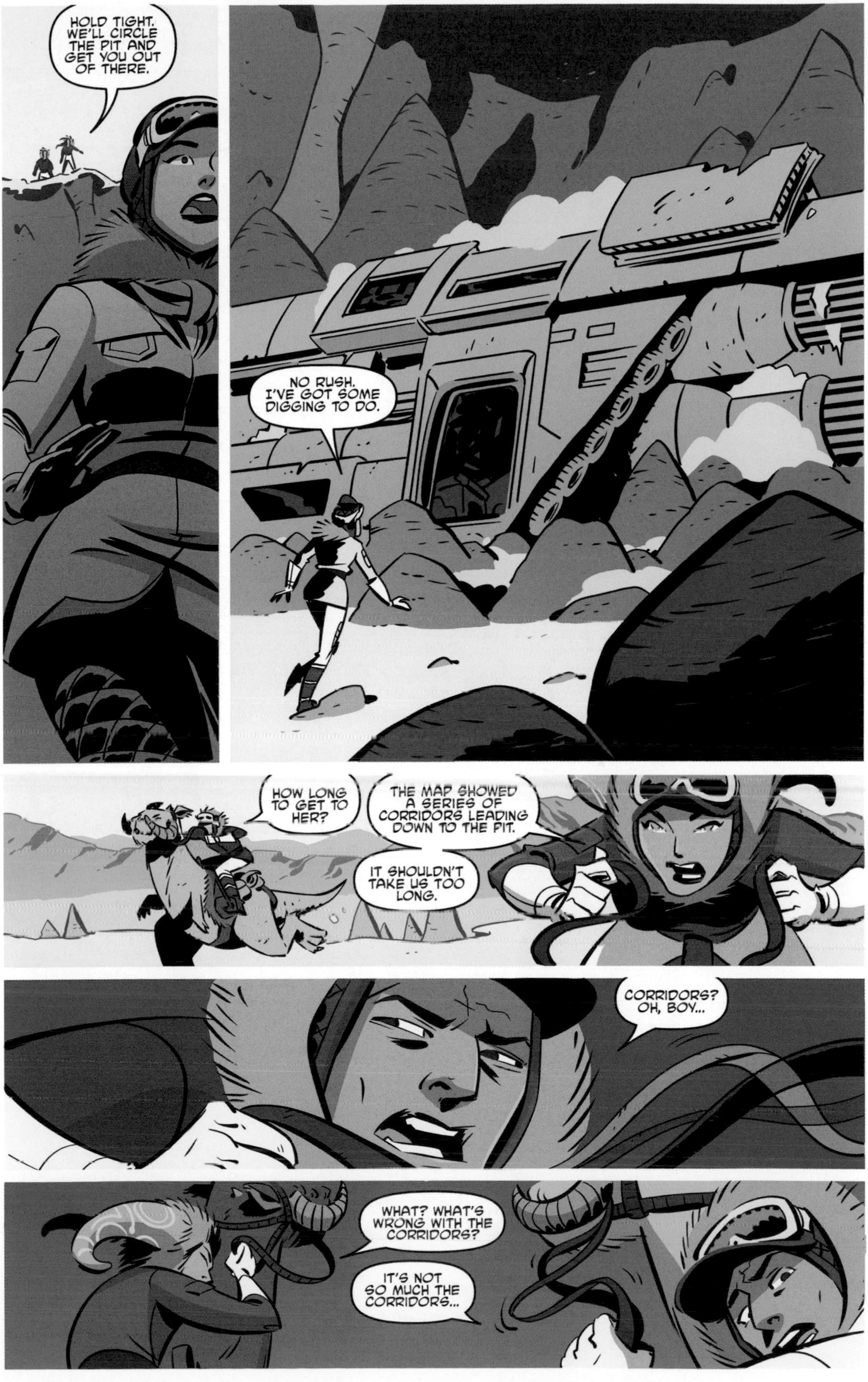
HOLD TIGHT. WE'LL CIRCLE THE PIT AND GET YOU OUT OF THERE.
NO RUSH. I'VE GOT SOME DIGGING TO DO.
HOW LONG TO GET TO HER?
THE MAP SHOWED A SERIES OF CORRIDORS LEADING DOWN TO THE PIT.
IT SHOULDN'T TAKE US TOO LONG.
CORRIDORS? OH, BOY...
WHAT? WHAT'S WRONG WITH THE CORRIDORS?
IT'S NOT SO MUCH THE CORRIDORS...

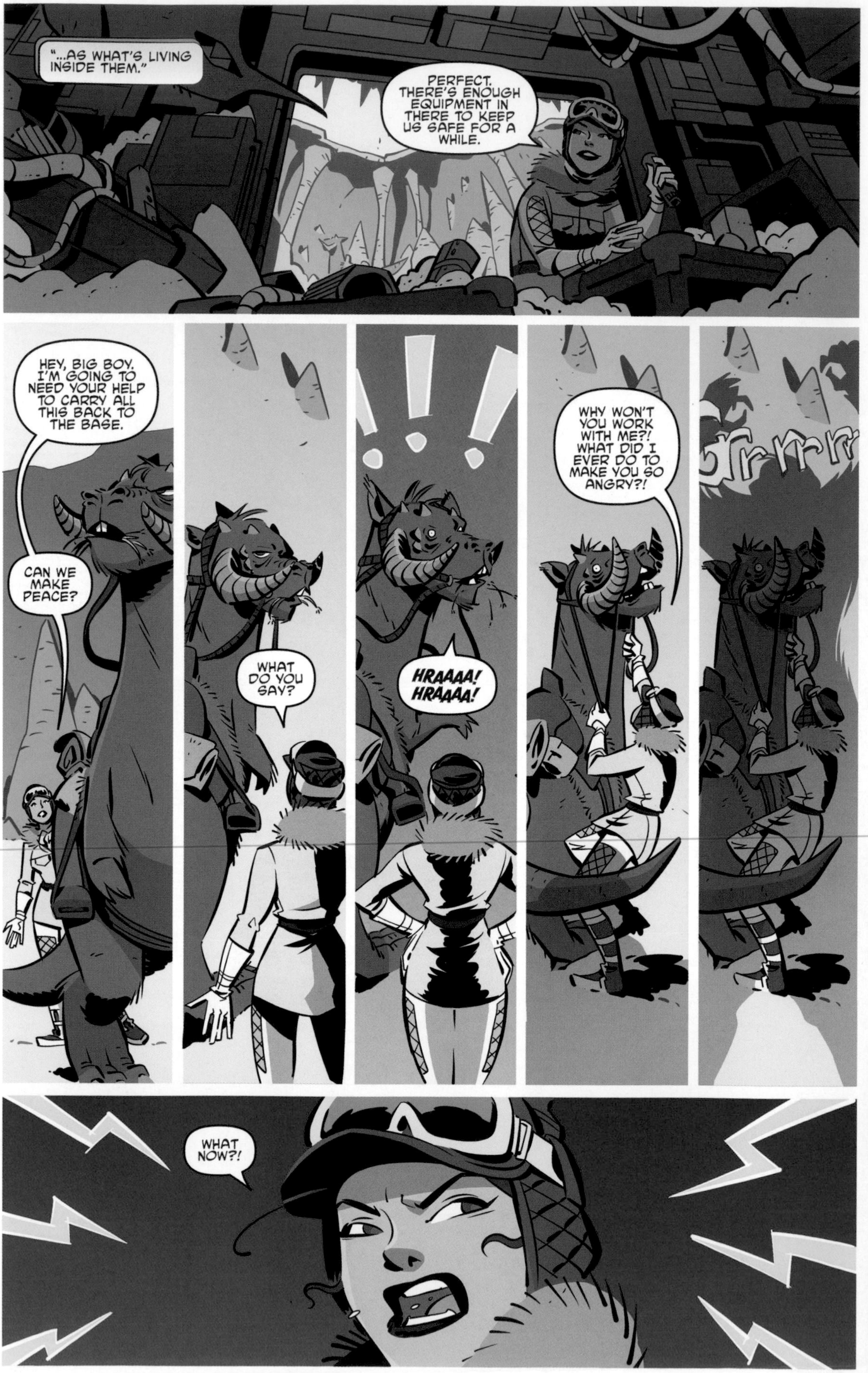

"...AS WHAT'S LIVING INSIDE THEM."
PERFECT. THERE'S ENOUGH EQUIPMENT IN THERE TO KEEP US SAFE FOR A WHILE.
HEY, BIG BOY. I'M GOING TO NEED YOUR HELP TO CARRY ALL THIS BACK TO THE BASE.
CAN WE MAKE PEACE?
WHAT DO YOU SAY?
HRAAAA! HRAAAA!
WHY WON'T YOU WORK WITH ME?! WHAT DID I EVER DO TO MAKE YOU SO ANGRY?!
Grrrrr
WHAT NOW?!

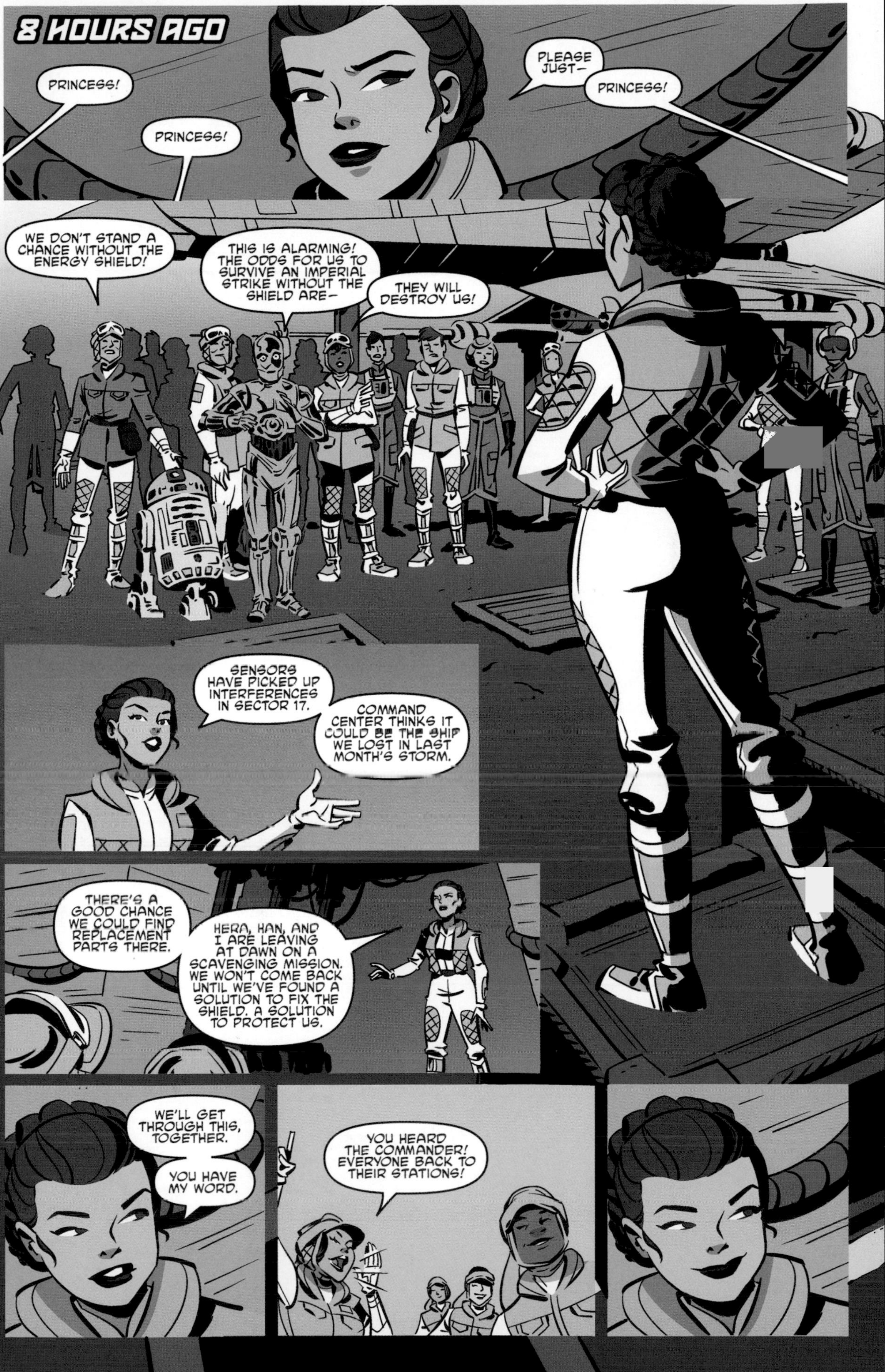
8 HOURS AGO
PRINCESS!
PRINCESS!
PLEASE JUST—
PRINCESS!
WE DON'T STAND A CHANCE WITHOUT THE ENERGY SHIELD!
THIS IS ALARMING! THE ODDS FOR US TO SURVIVE AN IMPERIAL STRIKE WITHOUT THE SHIELD ARE—
THEY WILL DESTROY US!
SENSORS HAVE PICKED UP INTERFERENCES IN SECTOR 17.
COMMAND CENTER THINKS IT COULD BE THE SHIP WE LOST IN LAST MONTH'S STORM.
THERE'S A GOOD CHANCE WE COULD FIND REPLACEMENT PARTS THERE.
HERA, HAN, AND I ARE LEAVING AT DAWN ON A SCAVENGING MISSION. WE WON'T COME BACK UNTIL WE'VE FOUND A SOLUTION TO FIX THE SHIELD. A SOLUTION TO PROTECT US.
WE'LL GET THROUGH THIS, TOGETHER.
YOU HAVE MY WORD.
YOU HEARD THE COMMANDER! EVERYONE BACK TO THEIR STATIONS!

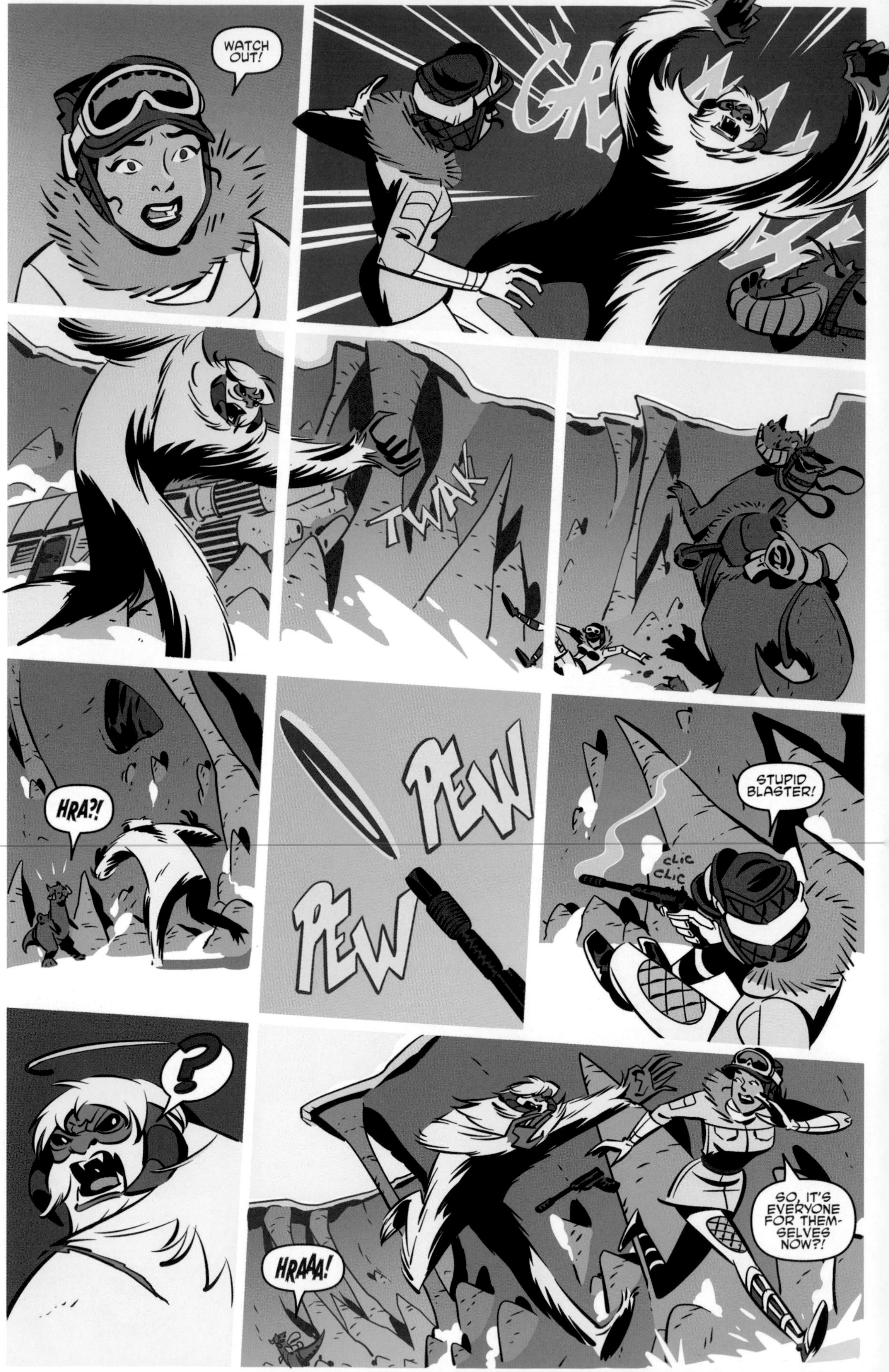
WATCH OUT!
GRAAAAHH
TWAK
HRA?!
PEW
PEW
STUPID BLASTER!
CLIC
CLIC
?
HRAAA!
SO, IT'S EVERYONE FOR THEM-SELVES NOW?!

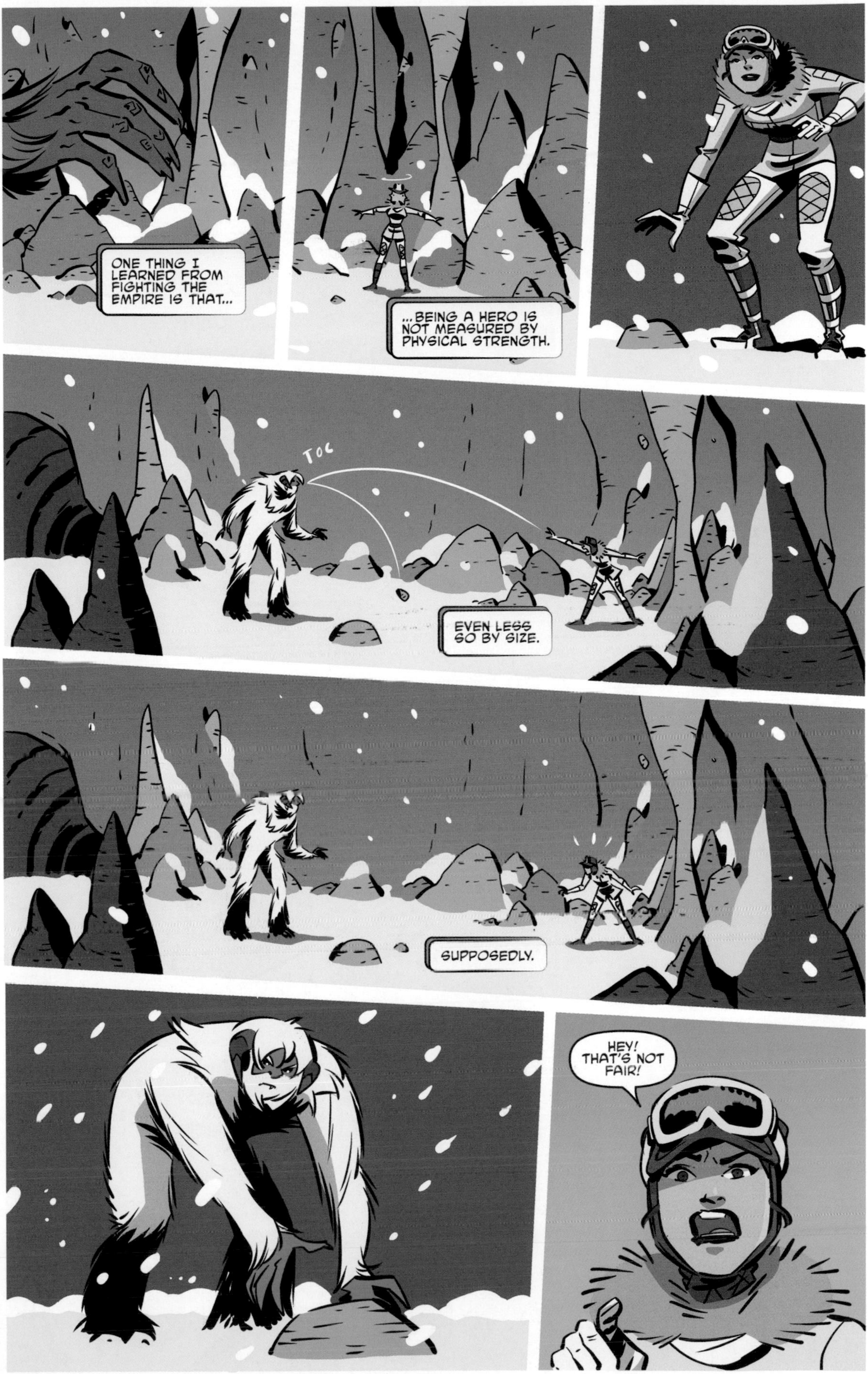
ONE THING I LEARNED FROM FIGHTING THE EMPIRE IS THAT...
...BEING A HERO IS NOT MEASURED BY PHYSICAL STRENGTH.
TOC
EVEN LESS SO BY SIZE.
SUPPOSEDLY.
...
HEY! THAT'S NOT FAIR!

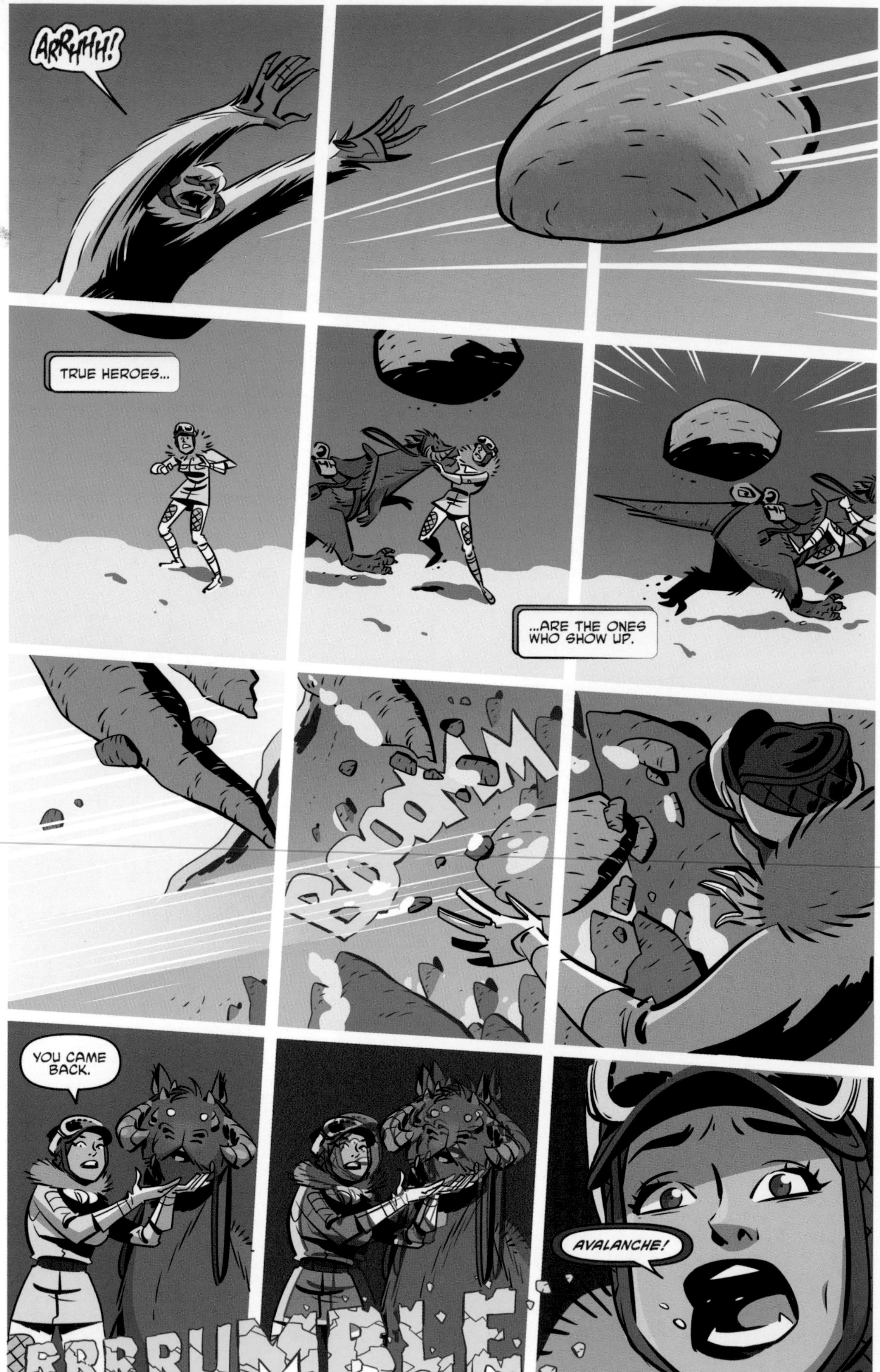

ARRHHH!
TRUE HEROES...
...ARE THE ONES WHO SHOW UP.
BOOM
YOU CAME BACK.
AVALANCHE!
RRRRUMBLE

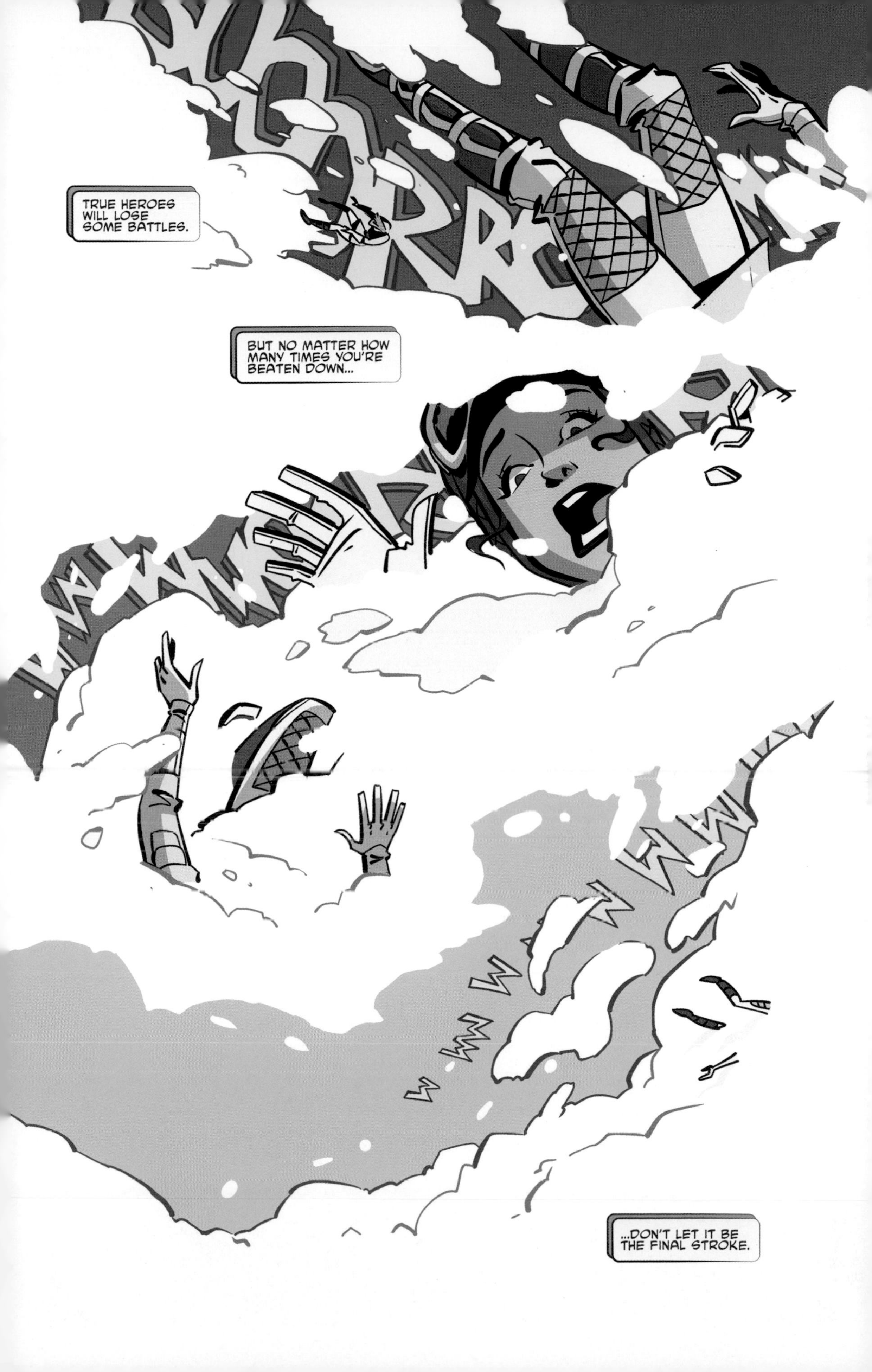
TRUE HEROES WILL LOSE SOME BATTLES.
BUT NO MATTER HOW MANY TIMES YOU'RE BEATEN DOWN...
...DON'T LET IT BE THE FINAL STROKE.

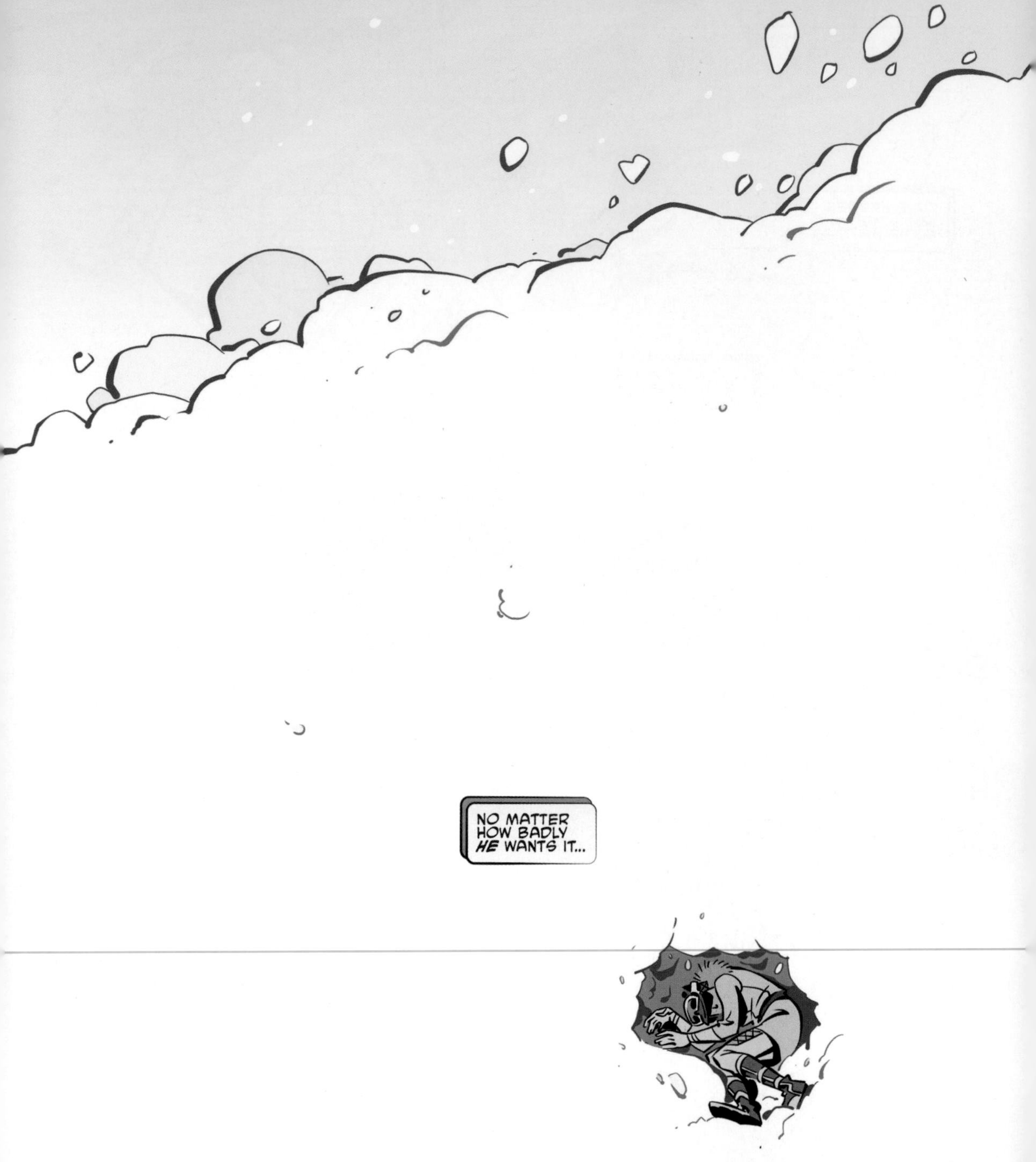
NO MATTER HOW BADLY *HE* WANTS IT...

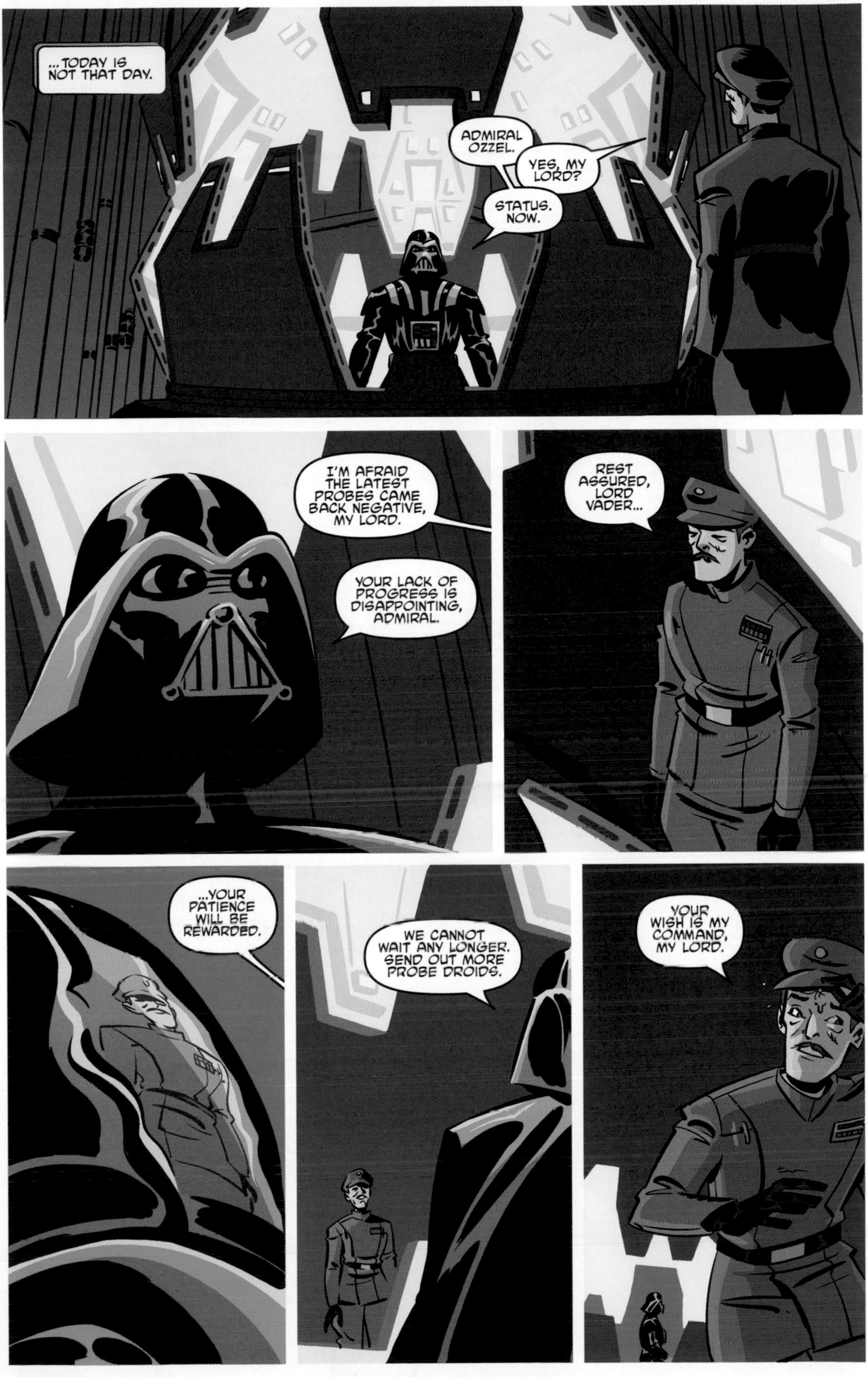
...TODAY IS NOT THAT DAY.
ADMIRAL OZZEL.
YES, MY LORD?
STATUS. NOW.
I'M AFRAID THE LATEST PROBES CAME BACK NEGATIVE, MY LORD.
YOUR LACK OF PROGRESS IS DISAPPOINTING, ADMIRAL.
REST ASSURED, LORD VADER...
...YOUR PATIENCE WILL BE REWARDED.
WE CANNOT WAIT ANY LONGER. SEND OUT MORE PROBE DROIDS.
YOUR WISH IS MY COMMAND, MY LORD.

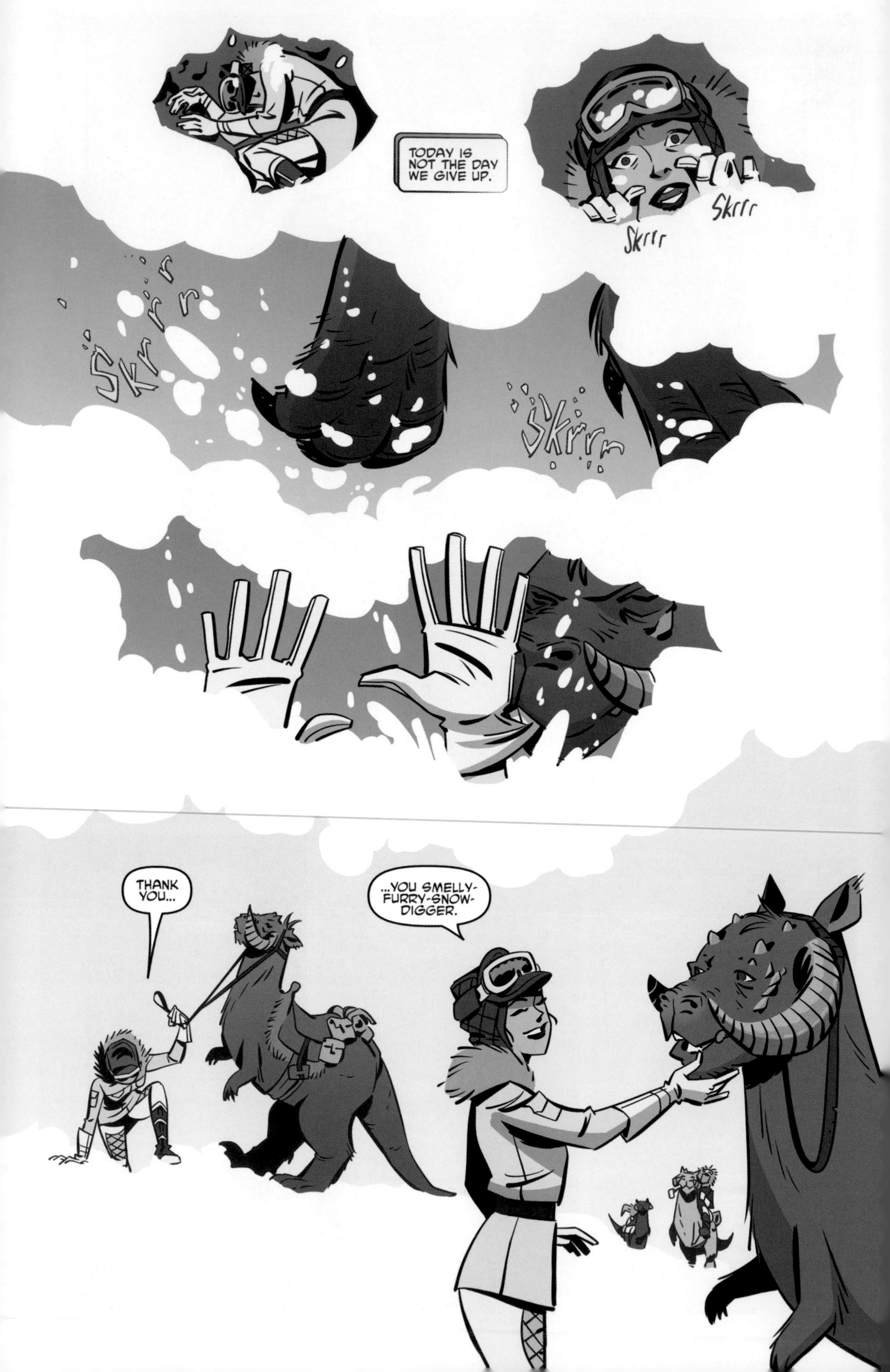

TODAY IS NOT THE DAY WE GIVE UP.
Skrrr
Skrrr
Skrrr
Skrrrr
THANK YOU...
...YOU SMELLY-FURRY-SNOW-DIGGER.

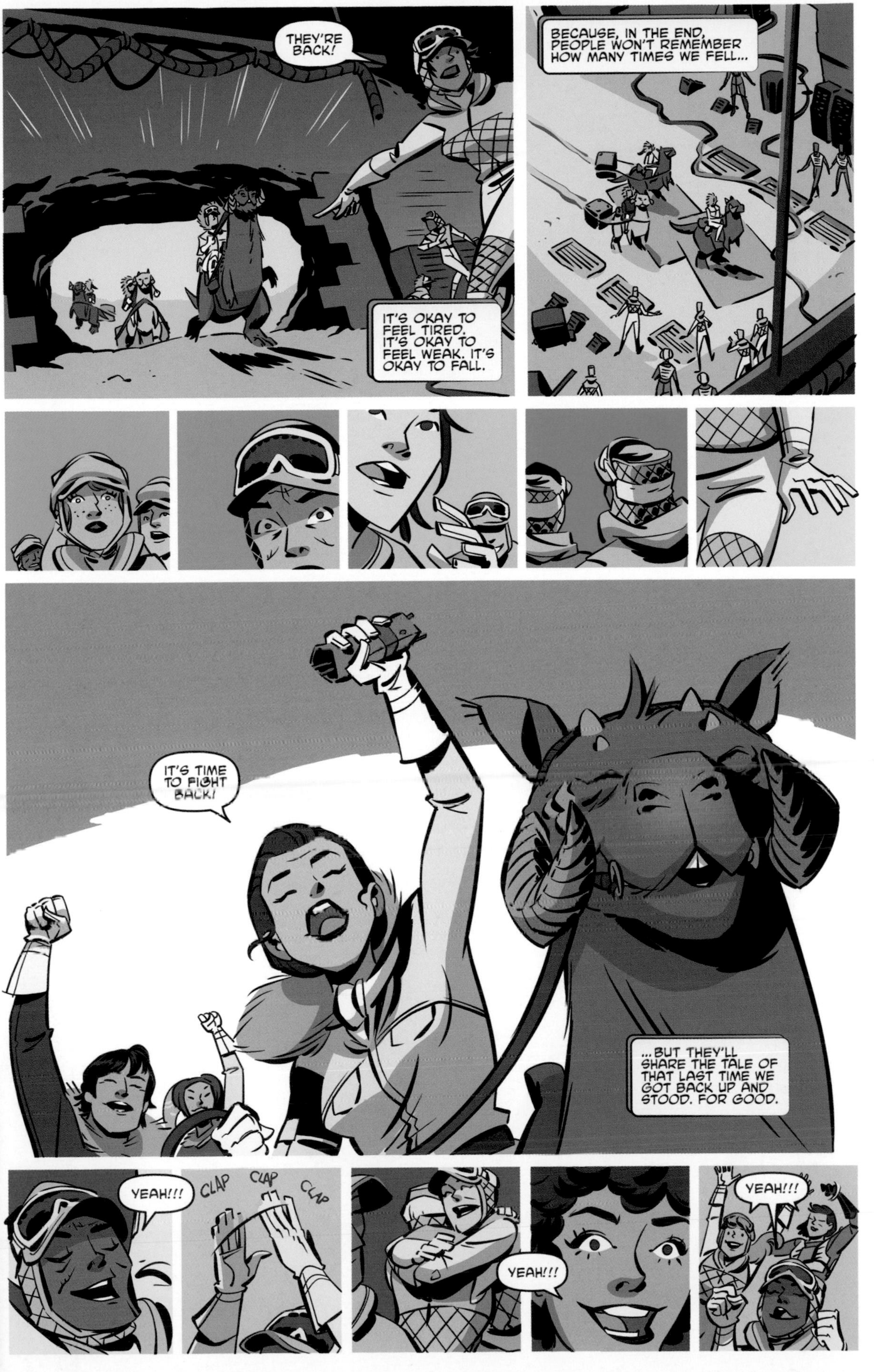
THEY'RE BACK!
IT'S OKAY TO FEEL TIRED. IT'S OKAY TO FEEL WEAK. IT'S OKAY TO FALL.
BECAUSE, IN THE END, PEOPLE WON'T REMEMBER HOW MANY TIMES WE FELL...
IT'S TIME TO FIGHT BACK!
...BUT THEY'LL SHARE THE TALE OF THAT LAST TIME WE GOT BACK UP AND STOOD. FOR GOOD.
YEAH!!!
CLAP
CLAP
CLAP
YEAH!!!
YEAH!!!

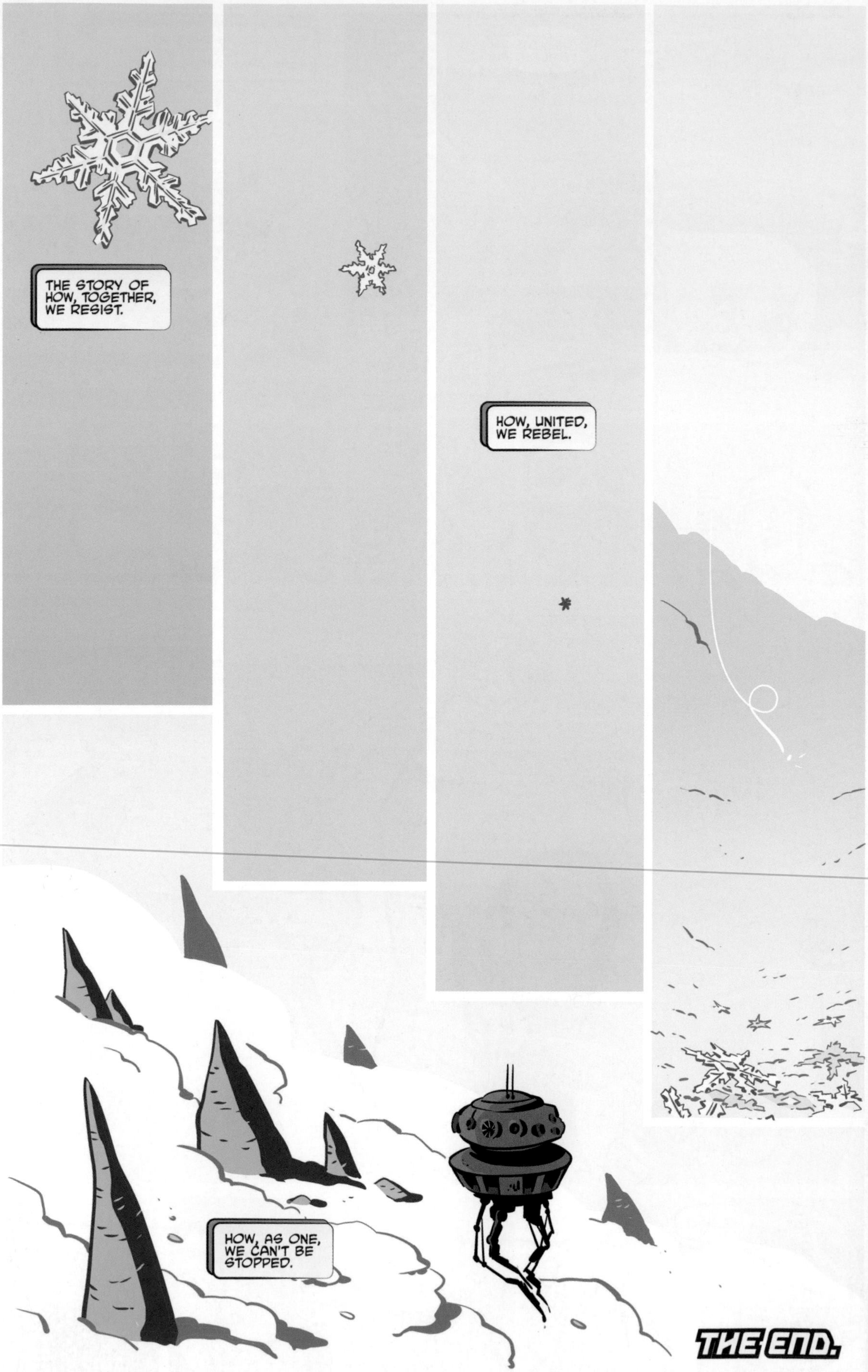
THE STORY OF HOW, TOGETHER, WE RESIST.
HOW, UNITED, WE REBEL.
HOW, AS ONE, WE CAN'T BE STOPPED.
THE END.

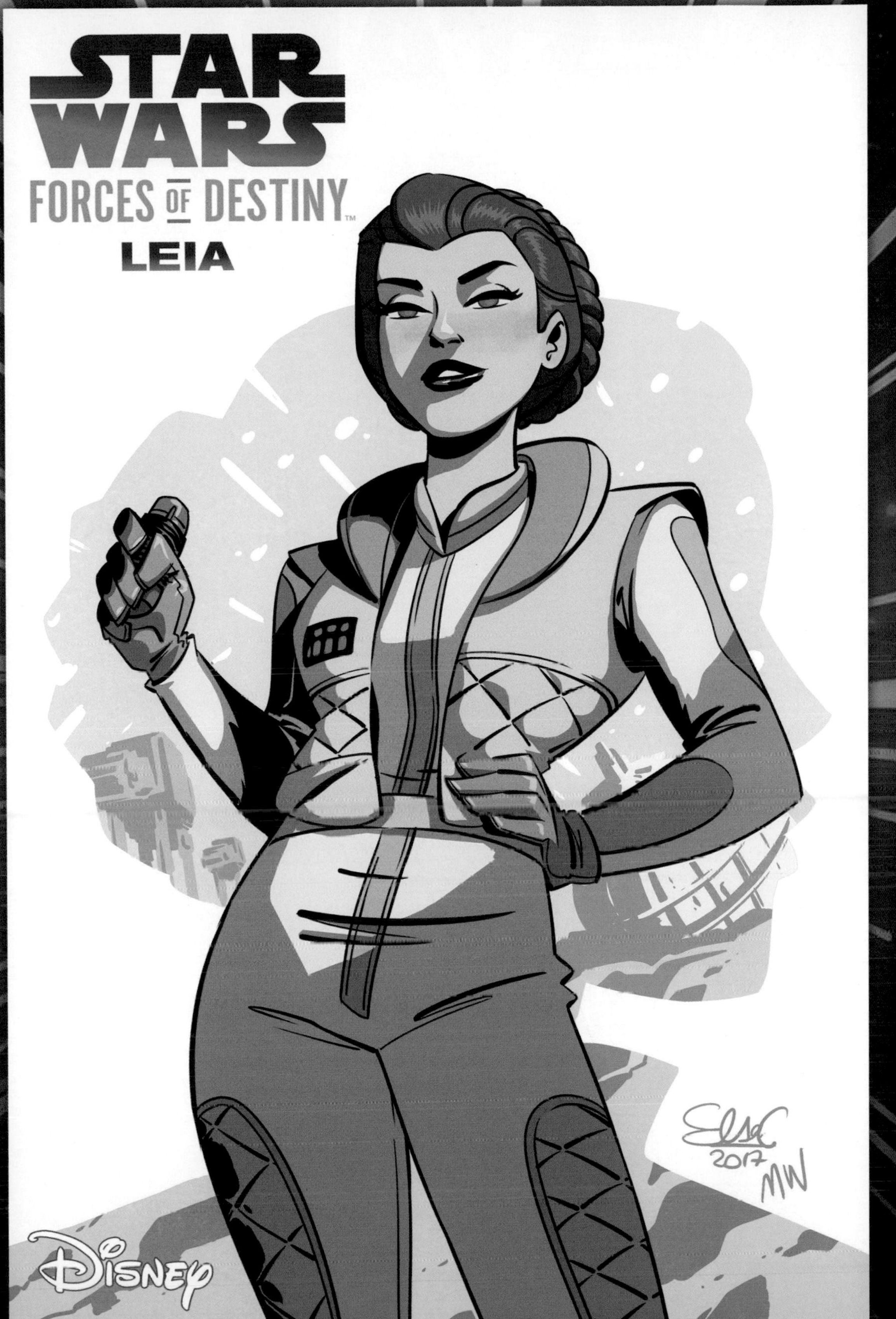
STAR WARS
FORCES OF DESTINY
LEIA
Disney

Star Wars: Forces of Destiny "Leia"

Variant cover B artwork by Elsa Charretier, colors by Matt Wilson

STAR WARS
FORCES OF DESTINY™

COLLECT THEM ALL!

Set of 5 Hardcover Books ISBN: 978-1-5321-4291-8

STAR WARS
FORCES OF DESTINY
AHSOKA & PADMÉ

Hardcover Book ISBN 978-1-5321-4292-5

STAR WARS
FORCES OF DESTINY
HERA

Hardcover Book ISBN 978-1-5321-4293-2

STAR WARS
FORCES OF DESTINY
LEIA

Hardcover Book ISBN 978-1-5321-4294-9

STAR WARS
FORCES OF DESTINY
REY

Hardcover Book ISBN 978-1-5321-4295-6

STAR WARS
FORCES OF DESTINY
ROSE & PAIGE

Hardcover Book ISBN 978-1-5321-4296-3